Published by Yeehoo Press

721 W Whittier Blvd #O, La Habra, CA 90631

www.yeehoopress.com

The illustrations for this book were created in photoshop.

This book was designed by Ye Si.

Library of Congress Control Number: 2020950330

ISBN: 978-1-953458-07-0

Printed in China First Edition

1 2 3 4 5 6 7 8 9 10

WHEN I'M NOT LOOKING

FARREN PHILLIPS

YEEHOO PRESS

*Someone who asks
BIG questions.

How many socks can you find on this page?

ROBBING A BANK

RIDING ON A

FIGHTING A

EATING A

OR GLARING AT A

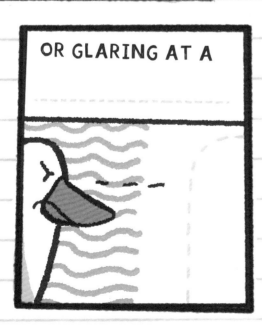

SHE COULD BE GATHERING AN ARMY OF DUCKS . . .

TO TAKE OVER THE WORLD!

OR **MAYBE SHE'S GROWING TEN LEGS!**

OR **WORSE!**

MAYBE SHE IS FARTING ALL OVER MY _____

Can you find ...

A microscope	
A shoe	
A doll	

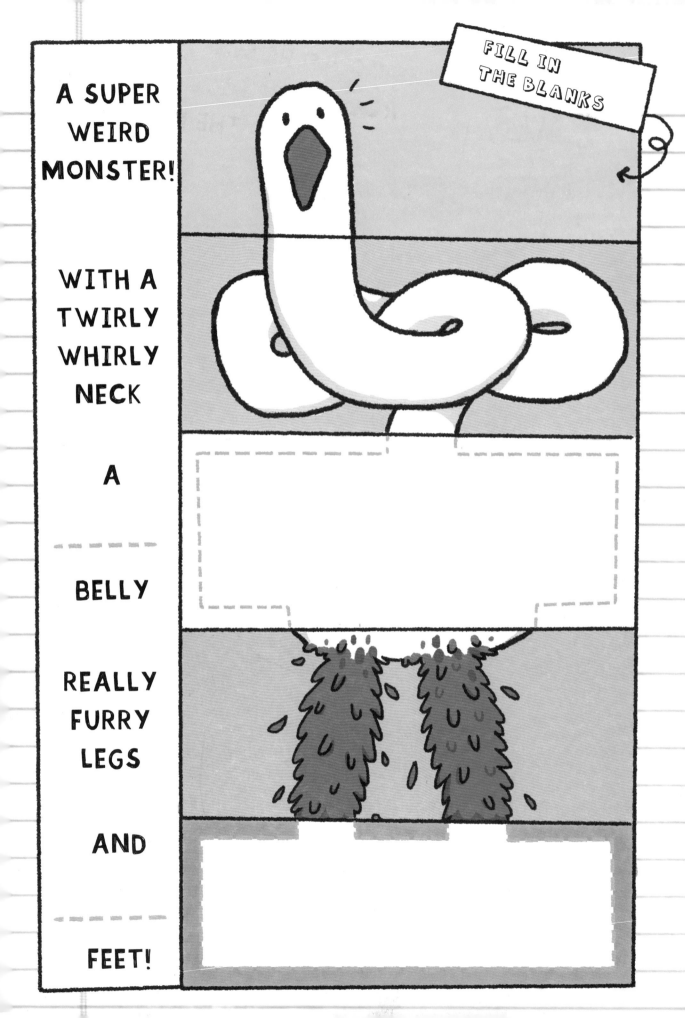

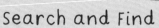

An
Be
Too
An e

Answer:10

How many did
you Find ?

Answer:15

Philosophy

Trapped!

Are peopl
scared
of rats?

YES	NO

Is she
plotting
against
me?
I just do
not know!

The humble city rat

Squea

Junior Physics
6+
By I.C. BUTTS

The biology of the
Rat